As Waves on the Sea

*A Charity Anthology for
Jersey Recovery College*

Copyright © 2024

First published in 2024

ISBN: 9798877042858

Cover design: Dreena Collins

Image: Sue Trower

With thanks to Sally Edmondson for editorial support

For the students, staff, friends, and supporters of Jersey Recovery College.

Preface

Producing anything creative is intrinsically personal.

When we produce fiction or poetry, we draw on our own experience, skills, knowledge, thoughts, and feelings. Even through the prism of imagination, or when writing empathetically, we do so from the heart. And in sharing our pieces publicly, we are exposing this to others. There is a vulnerability to this.

When we made a call for pieces on the themes of Hope, Opportunity, and Empowerment, we knew we were asking a lot of our writers – but never did we expect such a powerful, and sometimes raw collection.

There are pieces here on loneliness, loss, and depression. Likewise, we find poems and stories on hope, love, and friendship. This is a beautiful jigsaw of emotions, covering the whole spectrum of how human beings can feel.

There are few occasions in life when we make something wholly alone. We are usually working with the support or leadership of others, or with tools and machinery – even AI – to contribute to the result. This adds to that feeling of vulnerability; there's no one to hide behind because we did it alone. But there's also no one else to take the credit.

I hope those published here recognise and relish their own bravery and feel as proud of their work as we are. And I hope you, the reader, will enjoy this collection as much as I have.

Dreena Collins

Contents

Hope

Editor's Choice
Sunday Afternoon

Caroline Hepburn

"Green, blue, sparkles!" shouts Millie as she throws her unicorn across the playground. "What you do that for?" She laughs as I go to fetch Rainbow from the swings.

Just before I get there a little boy in a Teletubbies jumper grabs him.

"Mine!" Millie pulls one end of the unicorn while the little boy pulls the other.

"Arlo! Give that back to the little girl." He lets go and runs to his mum as Millie follows me back to the bench.

There's a gust of wind, and I pull her hat down over her curls.

"Are you cold?" I ask as I button up her coat. She shakes her head. She reminds me of a little doll my sister used to play with heart-shaped face, long dark lashes.

"Sweeties, Daddy?" Chloe's packed a tub of blueberries in Millie's Peppa Pig bag. She grabs a handful and feeds them to Rainbow.

"Look what I've got!"

"What, Daddy?"

"Chocolate buttons for Miss Chocolate Button eyes!"

"Yes, pleeease, Daddy!"

It's cold today. I'm wearing a T-shirt. I raced from training to pick up Millie. No time to change.

"Sorry I'm late," I told Chloe. "Just for once, could you please try to be on time?" She slammed the door shut, leaving me on the doorstep with Millie.

The sky's growing darker. I'm shivering. Still, it's better than sitting in my bedsit.

"Find somewhere better." My mother tells me every time I see her. "Work more hours." I already put in enough time. What with work, boxing and seeing Millie there's no time for anything else.

I'm watching my daughter on the slide singing to Rainbow when my phone pings. *Keep Millie's coat on. Make sure u back by 5.* I'm not going to answer. Don't want any more trouble.

"Daddy, Daddy, look!" Millie flings Rainbow down the slide. Millie's my world. My one ray of light in my boring, dead-end life. She's my everything.

"Sure you're not cold?" I ask her. She shakes her head.

If I didn't have Millie, I'd go back to Jamaica. I wouldn't stop to think about it. I'd leave this dismal place. When I first came here, I was so homesick. Stuck in a tower block, my mum worried sick I'd get caught up with one of the local gangs.

3

Jamaica's my home. I miss the colours, the brightness, the people. Most of all, I miss my Grandmother.

"Take Millie. Go, have a holiday." My mum doesn't understand. Chloe would never agree. Not in a million years.

"I don't trust you," she's told me. "You'll take Millie. I'll never see her again!" So here I am, and here I'll stay.

"Daddy! Catch!" Millie throws Rainbow, just missing my head. It lands in one of the dead bushes. I bend to pick it up, and Millie snatches it from me, running back to the swings.

"Daddy! Push me!"

I'm still pushing when two women and a little boy come through the gate and into the playground. It can't be? Yes, it is! I can't believe it, maybe I'm wrong, but it looks so much like her. The girl from college. Same dark hair, same cat-like eyes. I couldn't get her out of my head. My mate Joel used to tease me.

"Man up, bro. Talk to her."

"She won't look at me."

"Go on, bro! Give it a go!"

She was out of my league.

After weeks of thinking and even dreaming about her, I made up my mind. I was going to speak to her. When I got to college that morning, I looked for her, but somebody told me she'd left.

"Push me higher, Daddy, higher! Up to the moon!"

Leonie. That's her name. She looks just the same. Maybe her hair's shorter than I remember, but it's her. I'm sure of it. She's talking to the older lady. Her mum? Her little boy throws his ball. It bounces past me, out through the gate and into the park. Someone's left the gate open! He runs out onto the path. The road's at the end. He's running up to it. I chase after him.

"Stop!" I call.

As I grab hold of him, a man passing by picks up the ball and hands it to him.

Leonie's coming towards us.

"Mummy! Mummy!" Her little boy runs to her. "Micah! Never, ever run out of the park. I've told you before!"

He's about to cry as she holds out her arms to him.

She looks at me. "Thank you so, so much!"

"My little girl." I turn to go. "I've left her on her own."

"It's okay," she says. "My mum's with her."

Micah's clinging onto her as she hugs him.

I pick up his glove, wet and muddy from the puddles. "Oh, thanks. He's always losing them. Aren't you?" She shakes her head at him.

"Sorry, this might sound strange, but. . ." She pauses. "Do I know you from somewhere?"

"We were at the same college, but you won't remember me."

The wind's blowing her hair across her face. "I do remember you."

"Mummy, we go now." Micah's hopping from foot to foot, holding his ball. He kicks a pile of leaves and laughs as they scatter, carried by a sudden gust.

"You do?"

"I wanted to talk to you." She pulls a leaf from her hair. "Thought you didn't like me." I don't know what to say.

"Micah's dad," I hesitate. "Is he here too?"

"Long gone." She laughs.

"Same here."

"Give me your phone." Leonie holds out her hand.

I pass it to her.

"Now you've got my number. Call me."

Micah spots his grandmother standing at the gate with Millie. They wave, and he runs to them.

"Yes," I tell her. "I'll do that."

I take hold of the handles of Leonie's wheelchair and push her back to the playground.

A faint ray of sun breaks through the clouds, and the day becomes brighter.

Thanks to the NHS

Donald Brown

In the little world of Jersey
where we like things smart and clean
we planned a brand-new hospital –
the best that's ever been.

It would have to be quite central
with loads of parking space
but it took the people ages
to agree on the right place.

And when they thought they'd found it,
the building costs had doubled.
leaving Jersey's government
looking distinctly troubled.

It seemed for quite a time as if
debates would never end
until they settled on a plan
of just 'make do and mend.'

But there's another route to health
that Jersey can access
and that's to offer islanders
the best of the NHS.

In Bournemouth or Southampton,
Oxford and Cambridge, too,
Wherever specialists abound
There's a place for me and you.

The Hospital Travel Office
performs miracles each day
with a flights and pick-up service
to help us on our way.

And our doctors choose the hospital
that handles our illness best,
while the local Jersey specialist
provides the initial tests.

They sent me to Southampton.
To the cancer specialist.
who examined my left lung
And put me on his list.

The brilliant Mr Chamberlain
acted without delay
and barely three weeks later
I was off and on my way.

I lay on my surgical bed
the morning after my arrival
minus a cancerous lung
and confident of my survival.

The week I spent on the ward
left memories, I'll treasure
with very few moments of pain
and many more moments of pleasure.

The pleasure came from the staff
that ran the recovery ward
who gave me all the kindness
their generous hearts could afford.

There was Tep? or Dap? from Ghana –
a most remarkable chap –
with an easy style of leadership
and an eye for every mishap.

Sweet Elena from Romania
was never far from view,
whispering, 'Drink water!'
or leading me to the loo.

And Claudia from Portugal
grasped me by the hand
when I got in a terrible tangle
and showed me how to stand.

Then there was Marta from Poland
whose face wore a humorous twist
as she sorted out the medical tools
that dangled from my wrist.

There were Nigerians from Lagos
and staff from the Philippines
and a solid core of local Brits
that formed the cement between.

They were all at various stages
of a long-term nursing career
and it was written on their faces
that they all looked proud to be there.

Joannli from the Philippines
worked half-time on the ward.
while her husband nursed their baby,
whom they clearly both adored.

She seemed a happy person
who showed no sign of stress,
just proud to be a member
of the local NHS

We patients lay on our beds
In our spacious five-man ward
given all the attention

the nurses could afford

We were poked and prodded hourly,
with needles stuck in our arms
and our blood pressure recorded
to save us from further harm.

Some of us had cancer
and others had cracked ribs
and some of us made an awful fuss
and others were damp squibs.

I was not a perfect patient
especially at night
when on two occasions
I sleepwalked out of sight.

The lights went out at 10 pm
but I lost all sense of time.
Life rattled on its merry way
without any reason or rhyme.

But for me, it was a happy time
and I let the hours pass by
knowing that I was cared for
and I wasn't going to die.

So, thank you to the thoracic ward
of the Southampton NHS.
Of all the various hospital wards
you must be among the best.

The Daffodil Vase

Catherine Hamilton

As her fingers closed around the brass door handle, its metallic coldness ran through Helen. It collided with the rising heat of apprehension that fizzed and tingled its way up the backs of her legs and sidled up her spine. Momentarily overwhelmed, the chattering of the growing group of people behind her was submerged beneath the surging beat of the pulse accelerating in her ears. Her lips pressed hard together, eyelids tightly shut against the sensory assault; she forced herself to breathe.

"Mum, are you ok?"

Helen swallowed hard and looked up at her daughter. When had their roles become reversed? When had Chloe become the taller, stronger one? When had Helen become so small, looking up to her daughter for reassurance? Had it happened when Chloe's father Paul died, or long before that? Change happens constantly, and familiarity masks its progress. Helen couldn't pinpoint the moment the transformation began.

"Let's go in, Mum," Chloe urged gently, her hand touching Helen's, which continued to grasp the door handle.

Memories of Chloe's first day at school returned to Helen's thoughts. The child had frozen on the steps outside the door. The new uniform was too big, making her look even smaller, and bewilderment wobbled on her bottom lip.

Helen squeezed Chloe's little hand and assured her, "I can't always be beside you, but I'm always right here." She tapped Chloe's chest on the school badge sewn to the blazer pocket resting over her heart. The embroidered motto proclaimed, "res non verba" – deeds, not words. She'd given Chloe a little push, propelling her through the door. Waving goodbye, Helen had walked stiffly out of the schoolyard. Chloe hadn't cried, but it had been impossible for Helen to remain dry-eyed. Perhaps Chloe had always been the strong one? Refocusing on the present moment, Helen gave her daughter a nod, pushed the door open and stepped into the bright noisiness beyond.

The previous day, the lines of tables stretching down the hall rendered the atmosphere funeral. Shrouded in black cloth intended to show exhibits to best effect, the tables awaited adornment by competitors arriving to arrange their displays. Horticultural shows had been Paul's great passion. He'd cut his blooms and transport them carefully to this hall, the seat of the local Society, to show them off at every event. He polished his trophies regularly, relishing a sense of achievement from the number of times his name appeared upon them. When Helen cleaned them that last time before returning them to the show committee, she wondered who would hold them next, and she wept.

Returning home that day to the smell of silver polish still hanging in the air, Helen opened the back door, ushering out its unwelcome presence, and looked at Paul's garden, untended since his death. Leaves that hadn't yet fallen when Paul had died suddenly from an undiagnosed heart condition the previous autumn had blown into drifts. Rotting, they decomposed under unpruned rose bushes, littering the flower beds. A broken pane of glass remained unreplaced in the greenhouse, and the once neat edges of the lawn looked ragged while weeds grew on the paths. Paul would have been mortified but Helen still felt unable to pick up her husband's tools, hanging abandoned in the shed.

Coming home one wet afternoon in early spring, a shopping bag split as Helen approached her front door. Potatoes rolled down the drive and bounced into the neglected flower beds. It would have made her laugh once, but today, still stricken by the unexpected loss of the man with whom she'd shared so many years of her life, it was too much for Helen. Waves of grief engulfed her as the cold rain splattered her face, cooling the hot tears already flowing. She sank down onto the doorstep, hugging her knees, her fair hair, now silvered at the temples, becoming plastered to her skull. She remained there until the deluge subsided, along with her sobs. Drenched to the skin but somehow with something of the anguish of the desolate winter just endured ebbing away, Helen peeled herself wearily from the wet step and rose to retrieve her potatoes.

Under the shrubs, among piles of decaying leaves, were green shoots, buds clearly maturing as they speared their way through the detritus. An indignant anger flared in Helen. How was it possible things were growing? No time had passed since she and Chloe had cast flowers onto Paul's coffin being lowered into the ground. How dare anything bloom when she was still wrapped in grief? How could new life spring from the earth while it felt that hers had been buried with Paul?

Yet today, Helen was walking down the aisles of tables, not noticing their black mourning dress. Today, they were festooned with flowers, and a heady scent pervaded the entire place. Helen and Chloe reached the first-time exhibitors' section and clasped hands tightly as they read the certificate next to Helen's entry: a huge vase of Daffodils, their resplendent yellow trumpets raised, triumphantly heralding the Spring.

Helen's initial reaction, seeing the garden growing again without Paul and irrespective of her feelings, subsided with the irrepressible progress of the days. To her surprise, anger had transformed itself into motivation. Helen had begun tending and protecting the growing stems from the fickleness of spring weather, ensuring the Daffodil bulbs Paul had planted in the soft earth just a week before he died would flower to perfection. Her care, despite being a touch late, had resulted in a golden display worthy of any silver trophy. Helen's name would be engraved on it this time, many years after Paul had won it with his first efforts in the garden of their new home together. As her name was called and words offered in memory of Paul, Helen looked over at Chloe. Her daughter said nothing and did not clap. She just smiled and laid a hand over her heart. That said it all.

BUOY

Scott Temple

There are occasions when the sun's caresses encourage my eyelids to gently seal with meticulous patience. I relinquish all those cognitive impulses that so readily reserve my availability to life. Beach fires burn these soon-forgotten moments of intimacy, which only the privacy of sleep can offer.

I sail like a brush stroke on a painting, drifting from facts like a memory as it migrates toward the rhythm of a dream. I count my seconds close to me. I am older now, and my thrills are marked with vengeful clarity far from the chaotic tenderness of my youthful inexperience.

I have surrendered to nature. I was deserved of glory and my worthy life was just a momentary shadow in the majesty of the sun. I am taken from myself as the searchlights of my interior sweep the parties that have passed. My breath deepens on every inhalation. I indulge in the pleasure of minor consequences like a seabird on the tide, who knows what happens to the ocean after dark, or the ripple on the silent lake that travels like sound.

I have studied the sun, her strange silent devotion to life, I am calm as I await her invitation. An essential part of this vast and entire form of freedom, I am as close to death as my life can imagine; I feel at once like the seed that embeds itself in the damp soil, and simultaneously the rotting fruit as life decomposes from me.

I play out my life in the balance of these miniature moments, waiting in the grey areas, holding on to what I have left of myself as she exposes everything. It is during these occasions, if I am lucky, that I begin living the dream.

Hope

Sarah Strudwick

What is hope?
People say hope is this and hope is that…
But I say hope is colours like red, orange and yellow.
Can hope have feelings?
Hope is a meaning of believing,
It can be scary because you don't know where it will lead to.
Hope is impossible and love at the same time.
Hope is to fly away from things that hurt the most,
Is hope never having to hope again?

Hope

Laura Lee

We live in hope every day
At home, at work, at play

We hope for love in many ways
A hug, a kiss, an admiring gaze

We hope to live healthy, happy and long
We hope to conquer those roads that are long

We climb into bed at the end of the day
And hope God is listening as we pray

Healing is Messy

Rebecca Dominique Morris

Healing is messy, it's not linear
Sometimes things in your mind are not always clear
One day you're great, and everything makes sense
The next day you're drowning, and the feelings become too intense
Emotional healing isn't like a physical wound you see
Sometimes it just appears when you thought you were free
Maybe a trigger, a word, an action, or circumstance
Can 180 your actions and change your stance
Healing is messy, it's not as black and white
But you've got to have faith that everything will be alright
You've got to remember why you need to heal
Sometimes what we deserve is greater than how we feel
You've got to accept that the past needs to lie
No matter how much that may hurt and make you cry
Sometimes the things we hold onto aren't worth the pain
But it takes a while for the heart to catch up to the brain
Healing is messy, but then again so is life
Full of beauty, yet full of strife
Healing is messy and it's okay if right now it doesn't make sense
Just remember how far you've come from the past to the present tense.

A Meditation on Mental Metaphysics

Adam Freer

The light came up slowly, just a feint glimmer at first, as Ego became aware that The Human was waking, early as usual. Ego looked back to find Subconscious gone. Only seconds ago, Ego and Subconscious had been scheming, Subconscious's wispy tendrils wrapped around Ego's expanding form while it whispered conceptions and ideas.

But now Subconscious had moved into daytime position behind the rest of The Team, ready to manipulate and absorb in equal measure.

Ego's morning routine used to be so easy, but since The Human had lost their way, things had been different. The mirror had become particularly painful; the expansion of the waistline and general swelling of previously sculpted features was too much for Ego to bear. The rest of the home-bound morning was, however, relaxed for Ego. Their real-time to shine was on the morning commute.

Every tiny vehicular infraction would cause Ego to scream at Mood and Action until hand gestures and verbal questioning of parentage were dispensed.

Things had been deteriorating for The Human ever since Stress had declared they had had enough and started bullying Mood and Self-esteem incessantly. Everyone had suffered in this slow descent. Ego had tried to prop everything up, doubling his workload in the waking hours and plotting with Subconscious in the darkness. But the more Ego tried to quench the flames, the more violent and intolerable they became.

This day was to be darker than most. Ego had spent the commute (the parts free of road rage) inflating Mood with favourable comparisons to The Human's colleagues so that arriving at work, the more superficial aspects of Self Esteem were firing on all cylinders. The Authority Figure was waiting at The Human's desk; his face did not suggest the reason was favourable.

Sitting down face to face with The Authority Figure, fears were confirmed when they began to tell The Human that performance had slipped. They did not use soft language in this exchange, instead words like "lazy", "pathetic" and "unacceptable".

This was too much for everyone. First to crack was Security, who went off to a secluded area and rocked back and forth, singing songs from The Human's childhood.

Stress was next, screaming incomprehensibly, briefly muttering some comforting words before again screaming mostly in Ego's direction.

Mood fell over and stayed fallen over.

Self-esteem shrank almost out of existence.

Ego saw The Team disintegrating like a sugar cube in a steam room and decided enough was enough. They grabbed Action and Language and directed them to use some phrases The Human had never used before, phrases from Language's darkest depths. Language tried, eloquently obviously, to explain to Ego that these were the most powerful words, words with serious consequences. Conscience added that this was against everything the Team stood for, earning approving noises from the Moral Compass, which had until now stayed out of things. Superego, holding Id and Ego in reins, attempted to assert authority. But Ego vociferously waved away the protest; he severed Superego's reins. Ego needed the words to hurt, to scar, to soothe the wounds the fragile Ego had just suffered.

The Human was cut adrift on an infinite merciless ocean without a job. The job had kept The Human functioning on a basic level, offered some form of structure and purpose.

Bereft of these, days began to coagulate into a frozen mass of time, one day indistinguishable from the next.

The dynamic of The Team, already strained to begin with, became insidious.

Where years ago, The Team had worked harmoniously, dealing with obstacles with relative elan, The Teams situation room was akin to Lord of the Flies minus the exotic backdrop. Chaos reigned. Members such as Love, Humour and Aspiration had long since gone AWOL, but now Self Esteem and Security were growing conspicuous by their continued absence.

A small number of players now came to the fore. Ego and Id, unfettered by the now lethargic Superego, vied for dominance. Self-pity ballooned and blocked up most of the exits. Every now and then, even Schadenfreude would waltz graciously through the carnage, slightly perking mood up for a few seconds, only for them to crash once again to the floor where they would fester in the puddle that Memory had become.

On a cloudless and nameless day, on one of The Human's now rare forays into the outside world, a strange serendipity materialised. While queueing with a family pack of biscuits in hand, The Human was shaken from a daydream to find a familiar face smiling at them—an old friend. Conversation ensued. The old friend, possibly witnessing the metaphysical battle behind the Human's eyes, talked of struggles, of trials and tribulations, and finally of the road back. That The Human was still The Human, but after this, The Human would be stronger.

Silence. Not a solitary sound was heard in the situation room. And then, amid this shadowy silence, a light. A blinding magnificent light enveloped the situation room and the devastation these members had caused. Stunned by the luminescence, the members searched for the source. Self-pity deflated to such an extent that Security and self-esteem were able to enter and join the search. Mood uncoupled from memory who, while still ostensibly liquid, did noticeably increase in viscosity. It was, however, not until the light began to dim slightly that its provenance was made clear.

There, dangling gloriously from the ceiling, was an object no bigger than a ball bearing. They all stared, understanding as one that they recognised this object, as if from a dream of a dream. But as Memory finally solidified, the truth's full beauty was realised. Hanging from the ceiling, slowly growing, cleansing the situation room with the light it calmly and stoically emitted, was Hope. They remembered now that this was their missing piece, the glue that had always held them together, the oil which kept the members from grinding each other down. And in that instant, The Team was once again whole.

Hoping That Hope Never Runs Out

Helen Patterson

We are told that hope springs eternal, but I'm not so sure.
The eternal part I like. You've got to hope that hope will always be around.
It's the spring part that doesn't feel quite right to me.
Does hope come from a deeply, buried
underground spring that is hidden from sight?
Hope can hide from us; it can seem remote and even mysterious,
but for us to feel hope and
know it, then it must also be visible to us.

My hope is found above ground, out in the open. It comes from both
people and places.
It's there waiting for me when I pay attention.
Hope comes from a smile, a thoughtful gesture,
listening completely to each other, and being
understood. It comes from remembering and being remembered.
If I know someone cares
then I can hope for better days.

Hope is also found in places. In nature.
Every year, the leaves around us change as we hope
one season gives way to the next.
Nature tells us we are moving forward and invites us to do the same.

These things give me hope.
Hope to keep going.
Hope to keep trying.
Hoping that hope never runs out.

When Pain Becomes Purpose

Phoebe Pallot

I wish I could tell you that the rain is going to stop
God will take away your suffering, but I can't.
What I can tell you is that suffering produces perseverance;
Perseverance, character, and character hope.
This pain you are experiencing will become someone else's hope one day
Hold on. God is shaping you in this experience.
I love you.
God loves you.

Where Have You Gone?

Sonya Thrush

Where have you gone?
Where are you now?
Just a shadow that's left in times gone by.
You laughed, you cried, fun was your goal.

You partied like no tomorrow.
And danced until dawn.
With the winds of time, you changed.

Who am I?
Where have I gone?
I am still here.
Perception of me is different.

I am still me, but in a different way.
I still have dreams and aspirations.
My goal is not so high.

I laugh so hard; my tears are joy.
I can do fun things.
Party when I can.
Dance until dawn if I want to.

The winds of time will change again.
I will embrace it with enthusiasm.

Who do you see?

Little Hands

Carolyn O'Boyle

By the freshly painted gate, they stand.
Mum's clammy hand wrapped round the hand
that once wrapped round her little finger.

Oh, for those precious times to linger
on for just a little longer …
But would that make her any stronger
in this moment, as her heart
prepares to tear itself apart?

And then, old memories start to rise
of milk-stained clothes and half-shut eyes.
Endless days of unbrushed hair
(thinking people really cared)
what she looked like in the shops.

Drinking from cold coffee cups.

But so much time passed in a daze
and now Mum stands, choked up, amazed
at how the years have passed on by.

A silent tear drips from her eye.

But buried deeply in her being,
Hope erupts with words of meaning.
With steadied breath, she holds on tight,
"Go get 'em, tiger. Shine your light."

And with a kiss from cherry lips

the little hand begins to slip.
Her teacher beams from ear to ear
as waving hands then disappear.

And as Mum's tears fall to the ground,
Hope lifts her up and turns her round.
She sees Sun's light beam through the trees
and feels the warm September breeze.

Hope holds her hand in sweet embrace
'til little hands resume their place.

Social Generational Momentum

Mark Cowley

Michael is a laid-back 14-year-old. However, this story is set in the future. The year is 2071. He'll be going to bed soon. It's after 10.30. Earlier on, the family had been watching a famous documentary that was first aired in 2026. It's about the expansion of average life expectancy in the world in general, but more particularly in the most developed nations.

The showing of this documentary was the event that first highlighted a specific pattern of how life expectancy was expanding in developed nations and how developing nations were catching up in this direction. It was a topic of special interest to some people at the time, but as the years and decades rolled by, interest grew, and the reality of the situation became more and more apparent.

It transpired that when people eat a healthy, balanced diet through their lives, particularly from a young age, they partake in regular exercise, have an appreciation of nature and being outdoors, have a happy-go-lucky attitude to life, and they tend not to worry about problems too much, this combination of factors is the greatest contributor to a long life.

Another point that was first claimed at this time was that when couples who fit into this category have children, these couples often tend to have very strong, honest and happy relationships and a very close and loving family life. Such families are the least likely people to have unhealthy addictive habits. They also have a ruggedness of character, have some degree of resistance to illness, and are very sociable. Also, these couples often stay together for life, and their children are usually attracted to partners of the same mindset.

The final point that was made was not only do the children of such couples usually have a long and happy life in general, but they very often live a few years longer than their parents.

Of course, not everyone falls into such a category, but this documentary highlighted a group of people in society who are naturally most drawn to each other as both partners and friends and so from that point onwards, such people actively looked out for others of their own type.

Over the coming years, it transpired that such people often have infectious personalities and very good social skills. Society now had a social group that other people wanted to emulate as good role models. And of course, even poor, underdeveloped countries have their own equivalent of such people not being privileged to such long lives but still moving nicely in the right direction.

Michael had now switched off the light and settled into bed. He thought of the documentary he'd seen two or three times before. His great-grandmother was 92 years old and looked about 70 at the most. His great-great-grandmother was 112 and still living at home. His parents were in their late 30s and looked like they were in their mid-20s. The oldest person in the world was a woman of 137 and this record kept on being broken from time to time.

Life was good, and so were Michael's prospects.

He had a relaxed, secure feeling as he drifted off to sleep.

The Legend of the Two Serpents

Carolyn Coverley

A serpent hatches and ascends to the sky,
shimmering with flawless, vibrant hope,
mesmerising, and yet so very fragile.

"I will now be saved and prosper", they proclaim.

While ignoring the shadow egg
from which a dark serpent slithers,
burrowing down in deep despair.

Above some wait in patient anticipation,
while others worship the shimmering in the sky.
Oh, when is the miracle going to happen?

Below, the serpent rapidly learns computer code,
infiltrating every silken thread of the World Wide Web
with despair, hatred, envy and loathsome fear.

Some calculate the value of every shimmer,
wondering who they could fool to purchase,
while others claim it is just a delusion of the State.

The prophets of the House of Blue Shimmer
exalt the need to cleanse the House of Red Shimmer,
whilst those in Yellow Shimmer know they are supreme.

The dark serpent, so bloated with rage, explodes,
releasing poisons that pollute the whole wide world,
clothing it in shrouds of hopelessness and cold despair.

The vibration cracks the floating, shimmering serpent,
shattering it into shards of unfulfilled potential,
its iridescent lights go out as each piece falls to earth.

Bemused, they turn and ask each other:
"Why did I not receive the riches I deserve?"

Then, a few gentle folk in simple garb,
reverently collect both serpent parts
and combine them patiently together.

Possibly with compassion, kindness and love,
but maybe just something to do in a despairing world,
where purpose and meaning are obscured from view.

From this amalgamated mass, they fashion seeds,
which they give to those who are willing to receive,
with advice that each requires patient, lifelong nurture.
Each kernel encapsulating the potential for hope,
to blossom unblemished from the murky manure
so rich from the shadow of hate and despair.

Maybe now the Whole Wide World can flourish and prosper?

What if Hope?

Simon Nash

What if hope,
Was the gap between present pain,
And futures realisation, of coming age?

What if hope,
Was not the crutch of the weak,
But was hidden gem the adventurers seek?

What if hope,
Was the spark that drove,
Oceans' map-makers and wild rovers?

What if hope,
Was the ember that warms,
Winter's chills ahead of spring's dawn?

What if I could give you,
A spark from this flame?
A glance from this place?
A moment in this time?
A shiny splinter of life?
A sprinkling of calm?
A covering of warmth?

What if hope,
Was a gift of the heart?
What if hope,
When given, left more to give?
What if…
I gave you hope?

What if, in this moment,
Your presence here,
Gave hope to me?

The Antidote

Ellen O'Brien

Hope: *a belief or desire that something you want will happen.*

January 1st October 2022: 11:45 pm.

As my ride hurled through the air at an alarming rate through the midnight breeze, I suddenly felt a disturbing kind of peace with the decision I'd made to take this journey that evening. 'Out of the driver's seat...' a phrase I'd often heard muttered by old timers at meetings sardonically rang through my ear.

It felt as if my senses had been sharpened, and my mind had been cleared. *Bewilderment poisoned me against my will.* I hadn't intended to even get behind the wheel this evening, but my body had other mischievous ideas, with its dear friend liquid courage, and they had both involuntarily sent me here after yet another failed test in sobriety. *Despair was what I had subconsciously resigned myself to.*

Twelve counts down, and suddenly I was no longer even in control of this journey in front of me, let alone my journey of recovery. The dark irony of the dozen suicide missions I'd sent my mind, body and soul on was not lost on me, of course. A dozen being 12, 12 being steps, a single step being unachievable. *Back to the midnight hour, and the starlight spoke to me*, and yet I hadn't even considered getting behind the wheel!

What possessed me to make such a decision? I may never know. The moon shone down on me and blinded me in judgment on my course of action, and the stars sneered in protest alongside her. *Frustration coursed through me; had they not wanted me there moments before?*

I looked back on the trail my car had taken through my window screen; there were misty signs around me that seemed to be pointing to a tree that had been struck down harshly by lightning that had made contact with my vehicle. Was there a storm going on around me, or was it just the two bottles of whiskey I'd been drinking and the storm going on inside that was messing with my judgment? My hands had a sprinkle of a sparkling ruby colour to them. And my entire face seemed to be pounding to the peculiar beat of a nightclub I often used to frequent. *Terror...*

January 11th November 2023: 8:00 pm.

After my fellow members had heard my portrayal of that evening and the meeting finished, they started approaching me with expressions of awe dancing across their faces, implying miracles with their words and igniting within me a kind of gratitude *and safety* that I'd never experienced before.

Then, a man named John, whose face stirred at painful memories I'd long forgotten, came up to me and handed me a note. John spoke of 'how lucky I was to have survived my night on the road' and the insanity that had ensued. He gave me a wistful look and reminded me to 'thank my mother who'd found me in the hospital miles from home and who saved my life by coaxing me back to rehab'. *Therein, she gave me hope.* He ushered me to 'thank my old sponsor who was there for me in the blink of an eye once my car had crashed, slowly talking me back to reality.' *Therein, he gave me patience* and 'to thank the universe which had given me another lease of life.' *Finally, clarity.* I counted my lucky stars in agreement with him as he gave me a warm grin, nodded, then said his goodbyes. *Hope re-emerged through my body as I watched him walk into the daylight that shone through the doors.*

I looked down at the note John had given to me, flattening it out slowly. It unveiled archaic writing that referenced the conversation we had just had: '*the four horsemen of king alcohol and their antidotes, don't forget them, thank them*' on the back '*antidotes to the curse of the horsemen: despair, frustration bewilderment and terror... hope, patience, clarity and safety*'. Not a direct quote to the big book, but I knew the passage he was tipping his hat to.

It dawned upon me then that I had the antidotes that could devour the horsemen of this sickness, and thus the sickness itself, within my grasp all along. I was thankful to him for shining light on my own personal cure beyond comprehension.

I concluded that in one of my other 'lifetimes', he must have known me well enough to be acquainted with my lack of closure with the dreaded horsemen. But the memory loss during the untimely relapses of my past would be to blame for my lack of memory of who this enigmatic man was.

I read the passage below me that he'd alluded to, and I realised that the next step was gifted in front of me, alongside my antidotes, if I should accept it spoke of escaping disaster together. *Escape disaster. A wave of relief flooded me.* That peace that entered my body on that night on the road came back to me more real and smoother than gold this time. I now understood that married with the antidotes; this peace was the recovering alcoholic's reward for finally running the four horsemen to the ground. I escaped death, and much like the disaster I knew I had escaped that evening, I now knew this time deep within me, I would never encounter another chemically induced witch hunt for a void that would not or could not be filled by substances. I had been and would continue to be given answers. Antidotes.

Twelve relapses down, and the old sayings about the twelve steps came to mind, flooding into my consciousness. I felt a jolting, urgent sense that my journey this time would be, God willing, written by my hand and my hand only and not controlled by the distorted realm of King Alcohol.

Hope

Ann-Marie Hogan

A tornado whipping me up,
A tsunami crashing over me,
I'm losing control,
My mind filled with rage,
A tangled web of blinding emotion,
Fighting to find my way back,
Then the sadness takes over,
A deep dark hole, dragging me down,
All-consuming it numbs me,
Darkness, light, it's all the same,
Floating into the black void,
Nothing can hurt me here,
No pain, no joy, just emptiness,
I could stay cocooned here at peace,
But wait…a glimpse of light,
The warm glow of the sun,
Drawing me towards its brightness,
Faster now, the tingle of feeling returning,
No, I'm not ready to leave!
It's not safe out there,
But the light warms my soul,
What harm could this sun do?
Perhaps, just one more try…

Never Thought Much About Hope

Andrea Molloy

I never thought much about hope, but I hoped I would meet you
I never thought much about hope, but I hoped you would be
all I had dreamed of
I never thought much about hope, but I hoped you would
take my hand
I never thought much about hope, but I hoped we would
build a life together
I never thought much about hope, but I hoped I would
be worthy to become a mum
I never thought much about hope, but I hoped they would
one day hold my hand
I think about hope, and I am really glad I did because it
brought me you
I think about hope and know I will always be hopeful,
I was all along

Hope from Within

Simon Nash

That day when you asked me,
If my hope was sure.
When all that you could see.
Was a world that got worse.

'A crutch' as you called it.
'An aid for the weak'.
'Hope buoys up the spirit'.
'An alternate to deeds'.

You said I was 'hoping.
Instead of real facts'.
This ultimate deferring,
Of the necessary acts.

But hope is not wishful.
Or fantasised views.
It's not some strange ritual.
Words hollowed of truth.

True hope is much deeper.
A vista seen clearer.
An' if you're a truth seeker.
Then hope draws you nearer.

When hope's formed on truth,
Not the lies of the powers.
There comes inner strength.
Steels you for the hour.

Hope's testings in action.
In sight of how things are.
Hope draws the attention.
Gives agency, true power.

Hope

Sarah Strudwick

Is hope right or wrong?
Hope is a meaning of having faith in yourself and others.
It can be encouraging you to have strength when you need it the most,
Colours of hope to me are blue and white, like the clouds soaring through
sky on a clear sunny day.
Hope is like a mother elephant cheering on her baby to
walk for the first time.
Hope is love, trust, compassion and having feelings to succeed in
anything you put your mind to.
Hope is like a rainbow because it is long, colourful and never-ending.

What do you Hope?

Carolyn Coverley

"What do you hope?"
The rising sun demanded.
"For happiness, health and a perfect world, of course".
But the wind howled in laughter,
And howled and howled all day.
Sharing its mirth with all the trees,
who nodded their heads in agreement,
while whispering with much disdain.
"What?" I shouted to them all.
But they ignored me as the sun disappeared.
While the wind informed the stars,
Who twinkled with amusement.
In the darkness, despair enveloped me,
Until the moon just held me and gently said
"What do you really hope for?
Just look inside and see."
I did not know why or how,
but she stayed with me,
as I slowly paused and just let go.
Then, as the sun rose again, I said
"I hope to find strength and courage,
And my place within the world".
The wind sighed, and the sun blazed,
Illuminating a path before me.

Spring was Coming

Sophie Hawkins

Florence was out for her morning walk around the country lanes. The sun softened the frost. Daffodil and snowdrop buds appeared like unopened stars fallen in the night.

As she walked down the hill with her stick, she saw Henry out on his drive, crouched over the bonnet of his car.

"Hi," she said to him.

He raised his head over the open bonnet slowly like a tortoise.

"Hello, Florence," he said.

"Are you sleeping well?" She asked.

"Better," he said, "It takes you every night, whether you like it or not. And every afternoon now, too."

"Well, we're still here," said Florence.

"That's right. And every day, when it gets to six o'clock, I read the paper and have a beer. That's what I look forward to."

Their conversation turned to the young chap up the road who'd recently moved in until Henry said he'd better continue working on his car.

Florence walked on. She could be out for over an hour on a fine day like this one. The crisp air would have welcomed the neighbourhood out of their doors. Then she could do her jobs, have some lunch, then go out for another walk in the late afternoon as it's only forecast to drizzle at midday.

As expected, Mandy and Sue were out on their walk too. Florence saw them as she passed the postman's cottage on the corner.

"Hello!" They said brightly.

"Hi," said Florence. "How's your brother?"

"He's recovering," said Mandy, "getting lots of rest in bed."

"We're taking turns to do his shopping," said Sue.

"It must be hard for him and for you," said Florence.

"It can be," said Mandy. "But as I said to our cousin on the phone last night, it gives a good feeling caring for someone else."

Florence asked if they'd seen the new chap who'd moved in up the road, and they said he seemed very quiet.

Passed the school, Florence saw a few figures walking along the pathway. She thought it might be the young girl and her children, and as she got closer, she saw that she was right. The girl smiled at her, and the children jumped up and down in a puddle, their cheeks soft and rosy.

A joyful laugh erupted in Florence as she saw how the children forgot themselves in their fascination.

"They love puddles, don't they?"

"We've been here for fifteen minutes now," said the girl. "I feel stuck."

"They don't want to leave," agreed Florence.

"Well, at least they're enjoying themselves and not asking me for anything!"

"Except more washing," said Florence, as muddy water sprayed through the air.

"Oh, the joys of parenting," said the girl, with a smile on her face.

Florence remembered her own children when their cheeks were soft and rosy and then her grandchildren. She remembered as though it were a week ago because time cannot be seen as it moves, yet it's always moving.

Florence said bye to the children, to which one of them replied, and the other did not and walked up the hill back to her home.

The last two days had rained so much she hadn't seen anyone. It was days like today she'd seen shining brightly ahead of her during her solitude.

Florence thought about her encounters that morning as she swept the side of the road outside her house. Everybody had something to keep them going, whether it be 6 pm beer, caring for a loved one, or children's joy as they jump in puddles. She looked across the road to the daffodil and snowdrop buds filling the hedgerow. Spring was coming, as it always did.

Hope

Carol Rose Gaudion

Like a little sun inside us,
Always there, glowing warm,
Even when we least believe it's there,
Sometimes obscured, clouded over
By layers of hurt, pain, shame,
Despair, and by clinical illnesses
Of the mind, emotions and body,
Always, always, as the heart beats
And it still leaps,
Beyond reason, hope leads us on.

Time Again, a Song of Hope

Simon Nash

"Time is a healer,"
They all said to me.
My life is repeating.
Patterns I can't see.

A sprint to the finish,
Or just one more lap.
The uncertain distance.
Just say when to stop.

> *No one says, it's a dance not an athletic race.*
> *No one knows, you just go on at your own pace.*
> *None believe, that the cycle will ever turn.*
> *No one sees, and nobody ever learns.*

My life is a painting.
My work is an art.
This time we are waiting.
For the healing to start.

Here trapped in a feeling.
A cage of the mind.
But this isn't the real thing.
This imaginary bind.

> *No one feels, the harsh chill of this prison of mind.*
> *None can still, the turbulent spin of this time.*
> *No one thinks, there's another way for this life.*
> *I can see, the peace that comes after strife.*

And time is a healer.
And life finds a way.
There is a new future.
At the dawn of this day.

Depression Can Strike at any Time… it Only Takes a Phone Call.

Mark Le Feuvre

Then…

There I was, having a pretty good day. But then, in an instant, it changed. That is the nature of my illness… Depression.

I had a phone conversation at work. It all started well, but then the subject changed, and seconds later, they appeared — those very recognisable symptoms I know only too well. Those first warning signs that I'm about to enter into a depressive episode. Those feelings of contentment and being in a comfortable place a short while earlier have now been eradicated and replaced with overwhelming darkness displaying guilt, sadness and worthlessness. Basically, feeling totally hopeless.

A few minutes after the call, I phone my wife to tell her how I feel, but I've only said "hello" and she's already realised I'm heading for that state she's seen me in so many times before. I want to talk about it, but the words aren't there, but my very understanding wife listens and says all the right things to help me even though the moment or trigger has long passed; I have to dig deep and fight my way out of losing control entirely. I

51

feel totally unstable and try as hard as I can to remain looking as if there's no issue.

No one in the office realises the strife and agony I'm going through at that time, and if anybody asks, "You OK, Mark?" I always respond, "Yes, not too bad, just tired". Which, of course, is entirely incorrect as my world is once again in tatters.

I again call my wife. "I can't do this; I'm failing again."

After being together for 12 years and married for eight, she knows exactly what I'm saying and has been through this many times before. Knowing what to say, my wife says: "OK, M. I'm here if you need me." She goes on to say, "Maybe go for a walk and get out of the office".

This is what I do, but I know that these feelings are about to escalate, and I find myself not wanting to face the world or anyone. I need my safe haven… home. I know this will worry my wife, but for me, I need to try; I'm starting to retreat inward.

Back in the office, I look for a distraction, but the depression is getting a firm hold, and I'm starting to feel very tearful. If I don't do something soon, I will start crying, and things will take a downward spiral, ending up as a full-on depressive episode.

It becomes ever exhausting play-acting that I'm just tired and all is well. I'm just too exhausted and have no strength to continue. Eventually, all stability is lost, and after one too many episodes, I resolve to lock myself away in what I believe to be my safe haven… home. It will take a long time to get back to living again.

Now…

These triggers are ever-present, and a depressive episode can start without any warning whatsoever. In some cases, you won't even be able to pinpoint what the trigger was. Depression is so powerful it can do that. Also, not forgetting depression's best buddy: Anxiety. These guys tend to hang out together just to create further impact and destruction.

However, after medication and numerous psychology sessions, I'm now in a place whereby I have the tools to deal with these potential episodes. It's not just about recognising the signs but also accepting them and knowing what to do to stop myself spiralling out of control, which can be extremely hard at times. Unfortunately, you can't just flip a switch, and all is OK. I need to work hard with a lot of mental effort.

For me, the best tools I have at my disposal are the mindfulness techniques I learned from my psychologist. Something anyone can learn to do in minutes. I look for somewhere quiet or even go for a walk and sit again somewhere quiet. I initially take a deep breath in and slowly release, saying to myself, "You can do this; listen to your breath". More deep breaths in and slowly out. With every breath in, I allow those thoughts and feelings to enter my mind. It's in here that I have a little white room with a front door and a back door. Those thoughts enter through the front door, and with every slow release of breath, I allow those thoughts and feelings to leave me via the back door. All the time coming back to my breathing and putting myself here and now. More talking to myself in my head, allowing thoughts in and letting them go. The feeling of being here, now. I'm starting to feel back in control, and once again, I feel like I've prevented a full-fledged episode. This is my reset button.

And just like that, it's over. I'm able to continue my day in a similar condition as before the so-called trigger occurred. Instead of hours or days of feeling totally useless, a burden to loved ones, family and friends, it's all over, and we're back on track in a very short time.

The reality of depression is that it's always there, hanging around in the background with his buddy anxiety, just waiting for an opportunity to strike. I have depression, and I'm very aware of this. You wake up each morning knowing your day can change in an instant because of something as innocent as something discussed during a phone call at work.

What is Hope?

Andrea Molloy

What is hope – other than a four-letter word
It's an expectation, desire, a feeling of trust, and that is different
from person to person
It's personal and can't be defined or categorized
It's means whatever you want it to mean
It's as powerful as you make it
It gives people light in the darkest places, shows them the way
Hold onto it
Open your mind to it
Pay attention to it
Enjoy it

Empowerment

Empowerment Is:

Carol Rose Gaudion

When you catch a complete stranger
Smiling at you in the street
And you find yourself
Beaming back,
Part of the human race.

Is: when you don't smile back
But the offered smile
Settles inside you
And you feel, despite yourself,
Something good inside.

Is: when someone gives you a loving hug
And you feel safe
And warm and brave inside
And happy to be you.

Empowerment is:
When you have a lucky break
And turn it into many blessings.

Is: when battalions of sorrows come
And you are able to
Turn them into
Blessings.

Is: when you make a mistake

And there are people around
To support you
And you realise
That it's not the end of the world
And you can even laugh at yourself
And learn from it,
Turning the wrong
Into a powerful right.

Empowerment is:
Deciding to break a bad habit
Or engender a new, healthy,
Life-enhancing one,
And after many false starts
That may seem as many
As waves on the sea,
You finally feel you're getting somewhere,
And it's like you're wanting
To punch into the air
A single-handed high five.

And then when you want to break
Yet another bad habit
Start yet another new,
You can honestly say,
"I've done this before,
I can do it again."

Empowerment is:
When a golden opportunity arrives
To pursue something you've
Always wanted to do,
And you seize it,
Even with fear and trepidation,
You seize it,
And you have the courage and the help
And the hard graft and determination
To see your goal through.

Even the smallest of opportunities
Met
Count.

Is:
To fulfil the goal
And find it just what you desired
And more,
Knowing what you've done is good,
And will reverberate
Forever,
Like an eternal singing bowl.

Empowerment is:
When someone loves you
Just for being you
And you work out
You sort of love you, too.

Is:
When you do
Something for someone else,
From your mother to the planet
To a stray cat, or a human stranger
And you actually like yourself.

Empowerment is:
Feeling comfortable
In your own skin,
Even if it's being comfortable
With discomfort,
Accepting non-perfection.

Perhaps the deepest empowerment
Is being present
For the lifelong breath
And its rise and fall,
And rise
And fall.

From that
Arrives
Miracles.

When the Days are Short

Sandra Noel

And the rain fridge-cold,
I will tell you I'm staying put.
I'm going to bake the finest meringue,
ice a cake with indoor frost.

I'll invite you over for good coffee
with frothed milk and a generous
spoon of granulated.

We'll light scented candles:
winter spruce, cotton candy; shut out
grey-banner skies, snuggle up
under blankets, rewatch favourite movies.

But, should the sky decide to shed its winter skin,
I'll take you to the midst of tumbling snow;
arms wide, tongues skyward,
we'll catch as many flakes as we can.

Persistence

Caitlin Thomas-Aubin

Try it again,
the thing that makes you cry in the night,
because you can't get it right.

Try it again,
the thing that makes you dread daylight,
the thing that everyone else seems to get right,
but has you falling apart at the seams,
because your seams are stronger than you think,
and their 'seems' are fragile things.

Try it again,
the skill that grows slowly as days pass,
greening the grass on your side of the fence.
Persistence is your defence,
against your own lack of self-confidence.

Mother / Eyes Meeting

Bryna McGee

I often now
avoid your gaze -
the one i used to meet.
though in certain lighting,
for a second,
this is obsolete.

i would not tell you
of this feeling,
a painful recognition,
that both our eyes
align at times,
a generational condition.

the unkempt locks
which framed your face,
before i came to be,
i pretend to be oblivious of
in the reflection i can see.

if i look for a moment too long,
and allow my reflection to be clear,
i will see you in my bathroom mirror.
a fate i strongly fear.

In Control

Mark Cowley

Excavator operator
Expertly perform
Efficient activations,
And make it look like norm,
Switch on the engine,
Skillfully control,
And scrape up with the bucket.
Dig or fill a hole.
Approach with practiced skill
The job that you engage.
It's an interesting job.
It brings in a good wage.
It's a job for life.
You're steady on your feet.
You're financially secure.
That really is so neat!
You certainly feel the benefits
Of your occupational role,
And you like the feeling that
You're the one that's in control!

YESSY-IZZ ! The Support Dog

Catherine Hamilton

Yessy-Izz? A funny name to call a dog, it's true.
But that's his name, and you ask "why", so I'll explain to you....

He is mucky pup for sure, he digs some massive holes
In flower beds and in the lawn - he's worse than any moles.
He treads the dirt through all the house, those pawprints all are HIS.
He jumped on me, now I'm a mess, he's filthy, Yessy-Izz!

He likes to bark and make a noise, the doorbell rings, he growls.
When music plays, he stops and sings with whines and moans and
howls!
He's very loud, he's deafening, that racket is all his.
If he's excited, we all know, he's rowdy, Yessy-Izz!

He loves his toys, but he's too rough, and soon they fall apart.
He chews them, shakes them, rips them up. They're gone. It breaks
his heart.
Those broken bits lie all around, you guessed it', they're all his.
They cost a fortune to replace - destructive, Yessy-Izz!

He doesn't come when he is called, he just ignores my pleas.
He charges off across the fields and hides among the trees.
Adventuring is in his mind, and not a care is his,

65

He doesn't give one thought to me! So naughty, YEZZY-IZZ!

Dog food's not enough for him, he'll eat what he can find.
Tidbits from almost anywhere, he never seems to mind.
Smelly things he finds on walks and then the smell is his.
I dread to think what THAT just was! He's greedy, Yessy-Izz!

BUT...

If I'm sad and feeling blue, my Yessy comes to me.
He sits right down there at my side, his head upon my knee.
He makes me feel much happier, I give his nose a kiss.
He understands and wags his tail, a kind dog, Yessy-Izz.

People often stop to speak to Yessy in the streets.
He gives his big wide doggy grin to everyone he meets.
Old people, little children, they love that smile of his.
He's such a friendly Collie-Dog to all, my Yess-Izz!

He likes to watch the TV shows with animals and birds.
He scoots arounds when other dogs are shepherding their herds.
His funny antics make me laugh; he'd suit life in Show-Biz.
He keeps me entertained for hours, a real clown, Yessy-Izz!

He stayed with me when I was ill. He slept on my duvet.
He cuddled underneath it when all others went away!
He helped me feel much better and my thanks for that is his.
He's as good as any medicine can be, my Yessy_Izz!

Dirty, noisy, naughty - but Yessy's not all bad.
He's funny, kind and clever, just to see him makes me glad.
He's one dog in a million and all my love is his,
He's my best friend forever, come what may, my YESSY-IZZ!

Broken

Rebecca Dominique Morris

Just like when a mirror shatters and the pieces fall away
The things we deal with in life can get heavy some days
Trust is fragile and can easily fray
All the colours fade to grey
The world is full of people that are broken
Words too hard to say so they are left unspoken
As humans we stop to stare at our reflection
Pretend we are okay because we have learnt the art of deflection
But sometimes the pieces that shatter leave a scar that cuts deep
We all lie wide awake at night unable to sleep
We're taught that love comes forth like sunshine after rain
But we're not always taught how to process or heal from pain
Every human sees darkness and we all need a light that guides our way
So whenever you feel broken, speak up and don't be afraid to say
A listening ear and a helping hand may be all that a person needs
To plant happiness in those darkest seeds
The pieces may not fully repair
But having someone there
Helps the cracks to fade just by showing you care
A mirror once broken can piece together a new and safer reflection
Where there isn't the need for deception or deflection
So embrace and stop hiding your imperfections
Because life can get better when tomorrow becomes today
And a helping hand may be all we need to help the darkness fade away.

Be Your Wonderfully Weird Self

Sophie Hawkins

Evangeline's neighbours were away for the weekend and had given her the honourable task of looking after the cats and chickens.

It had been a day of ease and comfort. She'd been out for her morning power walk, fed the chickens and cats, then sat in the garden reviewing her music lesson plans for the weeks ahead.

The sun beamed down upon the grass and the pond in between the shade of the trees.

It was so intimately private, that Evangeline almost forgot about feeling uncomfortable in her skin. But as she turned her head to the side she heard the voice in her head –

Look at you, slumped on a deckchair with your jaw squashed and crooked. You look weird and swollen. Just thought I should let you know.

Evangeline tried to observe it. Those thoughts were familiar occupants of her mind. Her sister-in-law called it the inner critique, but Evangeline already knew the voice of her inner critique, and it would be there whilst marking work or, practising music or driving. This came from a different place and was like a fish slipping from her hands.

68

You are weird, yes. Her good friend agreed. *But you're not a danger to yourself or others; remember that.*

Evangeline sighed.

Ahead of her, the chickens scouted the area; every so often, they allowed themselves a one-second break to peck the ground.

Then, the wild ducks came down from the sky and landed on the water as they quacked to announce their important arrival. They glided so effortlessly that it was as though the water moved them.

Evangeline felt longing in her wild heart. She thought about what it might feel like to be a duck.

To be part of the natural world, to wander here and there, be carried by the water, to be in touch with one's most basic needs and to be free from the infinite perceptions of the mind.

To be free from the inner bully.

Because that's what it is, Evangeline whispered, *an inner bully.*

As much as Evangeline lusted over the life of a duck, it was a bit too light-hearted for her. Her heart had grown in the sadness she'd felt, and it wouldn't be as big without it.

She pottered around the garden, picking up feathers and wildflowers from the meadow patch behind the pond. She weaved them with vine into a headpiece and put it on her head. It didn't matter what the inner bully thought about all of this because her life belonged to her.

She raised her arms above her head, breathed in the forgiving air, and dived into the pond just like she did as a child on her 8th birthday.

The ducks took flight, and the chickens clucked in alarm.

When Evangeline arose from beneath the water, she had shed her skin and became The Swan. The ducks came back, one by one, and the chickens went back to scouting the area.
Evangeline swam figures of eights with her neck tall and proud, and the ducks followed her lead. She was at one with the water and at one with her wonderfully weird self.

Sun Threads Winter Ribbons

Sandra Noel

       through your branches
tempting early spring

I ponder your existence
               history
                   legend

       unravel the bindweed
     strangling
your breath

       and when the sky opens to warmer days
I'll absorb the hope in each morning

         watch you sew your green dress
           plump-purple your fruit

              flaunt what it is to be a fig.

Forgetting how to be Observant

Bryna McGee

All I wanted was for someone to find me interesting
from casual observation or just simple knowledge of my personality.
I paraded around as if I was eager to offer, to invite others into my
heart - to give them a place to leave their stories. But really i was just
waiting to be given to.
it's in a desperate way, this idea that somehow if you go to the effort of
remembering
every little detail of someone,
of forcing yourself to find new ways to see them everywhere you go;
you will eventually make it clear that you are a person worthy of knowing
yourself, remembering even.
but all this time spent investing, essentially waiting for this energy to return
to you,
you realise that you are not anyone,
you don't know anything about this person who deserves to be listened to,
memorised.
perhaps you're hoping that the more you concisely consume each
personality you observe, with a strange entitlement that was not yours to
have.
as you try to find depth in every soul you meet,
mostly those who would not have chosen to give it to you.
that one day, your own way of being - everything you've yet to find in
yourself, will be consumed in the same desperate way by someone else.
someone 'like you'.
so that you can be so understood, so seen, that you will feel like you are
someone who is alive, with hobbies and quirks and things that make you
different.

but you are not unique, almost less so now that it is obsessive to you, in a way that is performative.
you've spent so long trying to think deeply about yourself that you've forgotten how to think at all.
to enjoy something without first considering its impact on your personality.
you have none now, you are only fragments of all the wasted people you have collected.
most of whom you probably never knew anyway, as you were not trying to know them in the way it is to be seen.
But in the way, it is to conquer, to prove your ability to provide a value as a potential friend. partner, lover.
it is only once you have spared yourself, these desperate attempts at control of being,
that you can truly see another person.
look inwards if you can. Otherwise, you might never be able to lend your gaze to those who would
benefit, from the exposure of an unbiased perspective.
observing reality rather than collecting all those
senseless painted pictures.

The Demons Inside Me

Rebecca Dominique Morris

There are demons inside me, that I struggle with everyday
Nameless, full of shame, leaving me not knowing how to feel or
what to say
Their voices creep into reality, and leave me basking in insecurity,
and just make me want to forget
I wish my thoughts would just allow me to rest, please I beg with
regret
I listen, and yet can't seem to release from their grasp
I don't want to be reminded of the past
I've taken blame, and I've made my mistakes
What more do you want? Why there's just no give-and-take
Forgive me, believe me, I'm sorry. I can't change what's been
I've repented my evil. I'm not perfect, but I've admitted my sins
I've learned from the past, and I'm no longer the same
Stop, please stop doing this to me... this is not a game
Allow me peace, I beg, please, please let this darkness fade
I don't want to keep being cut by the same blade
You're no longer nameless. I've acknowledged your power
So please allow me to forget in this darkest hour
I've acknowledged you and given you space and thought
Please now, surely it's my time for self-forgiveness and
Now, it's my turn for me to find peace and allow it to be sought.

And Soon

Sandra Noel

When the moss is shouting
in the colour of warm,
I will sit in the shadow
of our wind-broken willow,
feel the sun pouring as water.

We'll nudge some branches
and ourselves back to life.
And you will stay close.
Your hands also know winter-hard soil,
the hope in the pillow turn of season.

Opportunity

Editor's Choice
The Why Girl

Sonya Thrush

No one actually knows when, where, how or even why it started, but it did.

When the girl was in conversation with people about certain subjects, she always replied... Why?

Where she was did not matter; there was always that ringing question... Why?

It did not matter how many times subjects were put in different ways; she always asked Why? WHY?

I will now try to explain to you... Why? When you are young, things are so fascinating that you need to know everything. Why things are made... Why things develop... Why you need to learn so much.

Learning is needed so you can grow; your brain needs to grow. You have tiny cells in your brain, which are like tiny pockets; those need to be filled up with all sorts of information and images.

When you take a photograph, you save an image. Actually, your brain works just the same.

So, by asking the "Why" question, it can fill up one more pocket.

Why do you need to know so much stuff?

See... Why? is going around your head again.

Learning can be so much fun, and we all like that, don't we? When you grow, you will have loads of information stored up in those pockets, ready to open just when you need them.

Why learn to read and write? Where would you be if you could not read your favourite book? The answer is you will not have a favourite book because you cannot read it.

If you wanted to send a letter or birthday card to your family, how would you do that?

Why? Because if you could not write, then you would not be able to say how much you loved them and how many kisses and hugs you would give them.

Life is hopeful for future "Why" girls, so keep asking the questions.

So, now, back to the why girl, she used to ask "Why" all the time. Which I admit can irritate people sometimes as I constantly asked... Why? Even when I got an answer from the first... Why? My advice is to use the "Why" question, but do not overuse it.

WHY?

Because... I am that "Why" girl, so I should know!

Money Sticks to the Fingers

Donald Brown

Money sticks to the fingers
in our society
If you want a home and a mortgage
just climb the money tree.

Banking's always an option
in a bank that can't go bust
or the more lucrative form of company
strangely called 'A Trust'.

It's one way of earning a living
and I wouldn't like to knock it.
You just have to slosh the money around
till some of it lands in your pocket.

Another way of earning
popular in our nation
is to go for a really high-up post
in public administration.

In colleges and hospitals
the files on your shelf
will help you save on your staffing costs,
and put more aside for yourself.

The Tories, in their wisdom
sold our assets to the nation -
Water companies, some prisons
the railways and some stations.

The worthy Richard Branson
thought the whole thing rather funny.
He gobbled up a railway franchise
as a 'licence to make money.'

As for the water companies
who've ruined our rivers and seas
they've raked in a fair old fortune,
which our government should seize.

Property developers
make fortunes by conniving.
to increase the value of their estates
by skilful ducking and diving.

And what of the value of the land
That should belong to the nation?
Some are owned by the heirs of King William's dukes
for their role in the Norman invasion.

Few of these activities
add much to the wealth of the nation.
We've lost the Victorian virtues
of science and innovation.

We make very few cars or aeroplanes.
Engineering's had its day.
And whenever we build a thriving concern
It's bought up by the USA.

But in the arts and sciences
thanks to our education,
we can stay among the world leaders
if we only seize the occasion.

The fundamental question
is the value we place on labour.
The economy's not just a Ponzi scheme

or a game like tossing the caber.

Selling our national assets
to a bunch of rogues and chancers
may make some people filthy rich
but does nothing to advance us.

In hospitals and care homes,
with human lives at stake,
Is it safe to leave the management,
to people on the make?

When they opened up the care homes
to private enterprise
some business folk stepped forward
with pound notes in their eyes.

With workers paid a pittance
for hours of sweat and toil.
the way some care homes operate
should make us all recoil.

There are no clear-cut standards,
to sort the bad from the best,
where the staff are like the nurses
that work in the NHS.

But the workers in the care homes
like workers everywhere
from teachers to farm labourers
Deserve a wage that's fair –

A wage that shows their value
to our society.
And, as for all those chancers,
that climb the money tree,

Why not Increase the higher rate
of tax on what they earn?

We might as well take advantage
of those with money to burn.

They did that back in the fifties
after the second world war
when the food on our tables was rationed,
for the rich as well as the poor.

Thinking Outside the Box

Sorcha Lenagh-Jung

It all started with an honesty box.

Joy and her husband Matthew moved to Jersey in the spring. They were desperate for a fresh start. Joy had been ill for two years. Although she could now see light at the end of the tunnel, progress was slow.

It was on the first sunny weekend after their move that they found Robin's honesty box. The *Jersey Hedge Veg* site guided them through unexplored lanes between potato fields and high banks filled with daffodils and bluebells. The box had a rustic, handmade look. Had it once been a cupboard? It was painted green, and three shelves displayed a variety of organic vegetables and eggs. There was a rusty metal box for collecting money.

Joy met Robin when she arrived at the box late one evening, and he was packing away the produce. Realising he was shutting up, she was about to turn away when he noticed her. He told her to take what she liked. She complimented him on his vegetables, and he smiled proudly. Joy noticed that despite being almost grey he wasn't so much older than herself. He had shockingly blue eyes that stood out in a very tanned face.

When autumn approached, Robin invited her to pick as many apples as she wanted. Delighted, Joy busied herself making batches of chutney and apple crumble. She loved Robin's smallholding. From the road, you wouldn't know it was there, but going around the house, your eyes were met by a group of raised beds. The wild grasses growing everywhere softened the look of so many box shapes. There was a substantial orchard along with several greenhouses at the back of the plot. It was like a rugged secret garden.

Autumn was Joy's favourite season. Gloriously sunny days came one after the other, with just the necessary nip in the air. It was a blissful time, but it all ended horribly. One day, the elderly lady next door called to say that Robin had been in a car accident. Joy was speechless. Passing the box a few days later, she thought it looked empty and forlorn. After that, they took their evening walks in a different direction.

As time passed, the news about Robin was encouraging. Soon, he could be seen shuffling about his plot. However, he was not his normal, cheerful self. Joy suspected such an active man would find it very hard to slow down.

"I've damaged my back," he told her. "My wife keeps telling me to rest. But what am I going to do sitting about all day?" He shrugged. Joy felt so sorry for him.

She was surprised when he asked if she would harvest his apple crop.

"I hate seeing it all go to waste." Robin pleaded. "I don't mind the wasps and worms getting some apples, but not the whole crop."

Joy said she would do her best, regretting it as she spoke. Walking home after the conversation, she felt useless. She didn't want to discuss her own health, but she had very little energy, and there were a lot of apple trees.

She was in tears as she told Matthew that evening over a drink. He scratched his head for a bit and suggested asking some friends to help.

"What friends?" She almost snapped. "I don't know anyone in Jersey. The only person I talk to, other than Robin, is the elderly lady next door. I don't think she'll be much help!"

If only she were well again, Joy thought, but 'if onlys' never got you anywhere. A violent storm crashed overhead that night. Joy slept fitfully and dreamed again that she was dragging around a ball and chain. In the morning, she admitted that finding help was the solution. Matthew suggested posting on the Facebook group *Jersey Ask! Advise! Advertise!* She and Robin would provide refreshments, and Matthew agreed to run a BBQ. Posting on the group and explaining their predicament made Joy cringe inside. She knew she was terrible at asking others for help. But she made herself do it.

A few people replied to her post, and she got several likes, but it wasn't clear how many people would come. She felt she should have asked for confirmation but had been afraid of sounding too pushy. She was anxious about how much food to buy. In the end, they just made an educated guess.

Joy was nervous on the morning of their apple harvest. No doubt it would rain, or they would be hounded by swarms of wasps. Probably no one would come, anyway. Then what would they do with all that food? She felt like a teenager who's afraid no one will come to their party. However, the day was a great success. Joy had a wonderful time, although she found it exhausting. Many people turned up, and it was lovely to see the children enjoying themselves. The sun shone, and many hands made light work of the harvest.

After a lot of internal struggle and quite a few arguments with his wife, Robin had to accept that he couldn't manage his plot alone. He asked Joy to become his partner in the smallholding. She felt excited but had to admit her own limitations. Matthew would occasionally be able to lend a hand, but would the three of them be enough? She doubted it. After some discussion and encouraged by their experiences in the apple orchard, they soon decided that a community garden would be the way forward.

They had a lot of fun inventing a name. Joy came up with *Homestead Harvests*.

"Homestead sounds American." Robin pulled a face. Finally, they rejected *Mutual Munchies*, and *Friendly Fodder* was born.

Friendly Fodder is still going strong. Joy has always credited her involvement in the garden as a major part of her rehabilitation. The project has also brought many new friends into her life.

Opportunities

Carol Rose Gaudion

Impermanence
Change
Mutability

Mutability
Impermanence
Change

Opportunities
For
Awakening

Love

Sarah Strudwick

Love makes me happy as a big red heart that has no rules flying through the clouds!

It means never having to say sorry because it's like a big hug to squeeze.

Love is a friend to confide in when your down and lonely.

Love is like a new bird getting his wings to learn how to fly with you,

Love is sweet, like sweeties to eat.

Love is like a horse galloping in the wind to his freedom!

Beautiful Land

James Sillwood

A crowd had gathered around us, a sea of black figures clothed in retro western fashion: faded baseball caps, t-shirts with washed-out logos, trainers, once white, now ingrained with the red dust of the land.

"Buti, you mean?" Jake slapped the side of his bare leg and inspected his open hand. He gave a grunt, as yet another mosquito escaped certain death.

"Yeah." I gave a quick glance at the man sitting between us. "Who is he?"

We were sitting around the rusty oil drum under the Baobab tree, its sparse branches offering an apology for shade under the vast African sky. My shirt was soaked. What the hell were we doing here? I read the label on the bottle in my hand: Bushtucker Lager, export only – keep refrigerated. While the warm amber liquid offered some consolation, I longed for the cool evening breeze to arrive.

While most of the crowd was squatted on the ground within the shade of the tree, the three men who had escorted us on the final leg of our journey held their position against a wall. I could now get a better look at them. One was in his thirties, and the other two who accompanied him were boys in their teens – neither of them hardly big enough to lift the Russian

SKS to their shoulders, let alone fire the thing. My own Caprivi, designed to stop an elephant in his tracks at fifty paces, rested against the wall alongside them. It had cost me a fortune, and I wondered if I'd ever get it back.

My gaze was met by a threatening scowl from the older boy. I quickly averted my attention to the gathering around us. It was clear that not one of them understood a word of English, and yet all waited for Jake to continue.

I had to get a few answers. (The warning that MPCI rebels were raiding villages across the border was clear enough). So why, at five that morning, had Jake insisted that we leave the relative comfort of our hotel in Accra to make a four-hour trip across country to this God-forsaken place? And what was so important about delivering the package by hand to a man who, as far as I know, had nothing to offer in return? All that afternoon, I'd been watching the two of them walk hand in hand, accompanied by the whole village, through the maize field, along the irrigation channel, an inspection of a new borehole and pump. Jake could hardly put two words of Ashanti together, and the man who had been hugging him and clasping his hand all afternoon communicated with him in sign language.

Jake took another swipe at his leg, which left a bright red smear against his calf. This brought about an excited round of tongue-clicking from the gathering.

"His real name is Butani Ruandi. Known him for twenty-three years now. Always called him Buti."

"So, how is it that you dragged me all the way out here?" I gave a quick glance at our three minders leaning against the wall. "And how the hell are we going to get back?"

"No worries, mate. They're here to protect us."

Getting information from Jake was like getting a visa passed by the Accra GAAU – unlikely to happen before the third attempt.

Jake looked up and studied me for a moment. "Listen, mate; this is the only village around here which can supply the rebs with food. They know about fighting, but not the first thing about farming. I've been up here twice since the place was taken over, and there's not been a single murder or rape. It's a pact."

I accepted his assurance for now. "And what's with the package?" I asked.

There was a pause as Jake leaned back against the tree and took a swig from his bottle. "Third of this year's wages." The words were tossed away so casually that it took a while for me to catch them.

"A third? Of your salary? Jesus! You're joking, man! What the hell for?"

Jake rested his foot on the oil drum, and I could hear a murmuring from the wall behind us.

"See those two marks?" Jake pointed to his ankle.

Two white pinpoints stood out against his tanned skin.

"Demon – Bush Viper."

These words produced more tongue-clicking from the crowd.

"I was nineteen. On my first trip out here. A bit green… and very stupid, I guess." Jake nodded towards the man sitting between us. "If Buti hadn't found me, I wouldn't be here today." He pointed towards the line of shimmering hills to the east of the village. "It happened over that ridge. Carried me on his back for six miles; medic just saved me in time. So, mate, a share of my wages each year is hardly a sum to die for. What do you think?"

I let out a long whistle, which immediately triggered a choral response from the crowd. The sound surged towards a climax, then followed a series of sharp metallic clicks from the trio at the rear. A few heads turned. The whistling quickly died. I looked over my shoulder towards the percussion section and was greeted with three raised rifles, their barrels aimed towards us.

I steadied my voice. "So," I continued, "Thanks to your generosity, I guess this is the only place around here which has a regular supply of water through the dry season?"

Jake seemed unmoved. He raised his hand and held it at striking distance above his thigh.

I held my breath and dared not look over my shoulder.

"Yeah," said Jake. "And thanks to Buti's generosity, a regular supply of bloody mosquitoes!" His hand came down with a resounding slap.

He missed!

The crowd was silent.

The rebels had gone.

About Jersey Recovery College

Founded on the principles of Hope, Opportunity, and Empowerment in 2017, Jersey Recovery College (JRC) is a charity providing free mental health education for local islanders.

We offer education and training opportunities to people experiencing mental health difficulties and the family, friends and professionals who support them. In addition, we have a Mental Health at Work provision, providing businesses with the tools they need to ensure their workplace is healthy for all.

Our courses support adults in enhancing their knowledge and understanding of mental health conditions, recovery, wellbeing, and life skills.

We are passionate about co-production. Every community course is co-designed and co-delivered by a peer facilitator with lived experience and a practitioner facilitator with professional expertise in the topic area.

JRC appreciates all donations and offers of support – big or small.

Contact us at: hello@recovery.je

Printed in Great Britain
by Amazon

38754376R00057